No Swimming in Dark Pond

and Other Chilling Tales

No
Swimming
in Dark Pond
and Other Chilling Tales

JUDITH GOROG

Philomel Books • New York

First published by Philomel Books,
a division of The Putnam Publishing Group
51 Madison Avenue, New York, NY 10010.
Printed and bound in the United States of America.
Text copyright © 1987 by Judith Gorog.
Afterword by Dr. Caroline Bauer
Copyright © 1987 by Philomel Books
Cover art copyright © 1987 by Richard Egielski.
Design by Alice Lee Groton. All rights reserved.
Library of Congress Cataloging-in-Publication Data
Gorog, Judith. No Swimming in Dark Pond and other chilling tales.
Contents: No swimming in Dark Pond—The notebook—How
I kill my stepmothers—[etc.] 1. Horror tales,
American. 2. Short stories, American.
[1. Horror stories. 2. Short stories.] I. Title.
PZ7.G673No 1987 [Fic] 86-22586
ISBN 0-399-21418-6
First impression

In Memory of
my brother, Harry Allen

Contents

No Swimming
in Dark Pond

Matilda was living in that trailer park up in Bloomingdale when her husband left her. Until then, nobody thought she had two sticks to rub together, but as soon as he was gone, she bought herself an old shack with a few acres out along the shore of the pond, the one called Dark Pond.

It first got that name because it was so long and narrow, with dense forest right down to the water's edge. Shadows kept the water dark both night and day, except when the sun or moon was directly overhead. Now, because of Matilda, the name is darker still.

Hardly anybody lived on the shore of Dark Pond ever, even when Matilda first moved there. It had more than the usual amount of that high-mountain forest swamp you find up in the Adirondacks, and it was hard to get there. Just like any other pond up here, it had voracious black flies in May and June, and mosquitoes just as hungry nearly till snowfall; but even so, Dark Pond was pretty.

Old Matilda, she just loved it. Back in that trailer park, she had been a puffy, fat woman. But out in the woods she got all lean and leathery. The old gal had no electricity, no pump even. She cut her firewood from fallen trees and bathed every day in the chill water of Dark Pond. Matilda had never been so happy—except for one thing.

People. There weren't many, but Matilda complained. At first, complaining was all she did.

Matilda said the people who came to camp or fish left so much garbage behind them that she had to spend every living minute cleaning it up and hauling it out.

Matilda started lecturing everybody she met, and it did seem to help keep the boat landing and campsites clean. People never knew when the old girl would pop up and start in on them! After a while, though, anyone could tell it wasn't the trash that made Matilda so crabby; she wanted that pond for herself alone.

For a start she let out here and there that "something" was in Dark Pond. She said the something moved, splashed, and ground its teeth at night so the sound echoed over the quiet water of Dark Pond. Before long, others heard it too, the sound of something big grinding its teeth at night at Dark Pond. People even came to hear it, which made Matilda furious.

Soon, fishermen were claiming something was stealing their catches, something that left nothing but bloody shreds on the line.

Matilda was a strong, silent swimmer. It was nothing for her to go underwater to put a shredded fish on the line of someone dozing in his rowboat. The first time she did it, Matilda felt something small swim past her leg, brushing it lightly.

Matilda next went after the swimmers, approaching silently underwater to grab a heel, to pull them under, just for an instant, just long enough for the swimmer to be afraid.

All those tricks worked. Dark Pond just wasn't the first choice of folks going camping, fishing, or swimming. But still Matilda wasn't satisfied. Her ambition had grown. She could not bear to see another living soul visit Dark Pond.

The fewer the people who came to fish or swim, the meaner Matilda was when she got to them. Matilda pinched or scratched the swimmers she pulled under, sometimes drawing blood, all to frighten them, to convince everyone that "something" was in Dark Pond.

And each time Matilda attacked a swimmer, she felt something swim past her leg, brushing it lightly.

But nothing frightened Matilda. She swam every day in Dark Pond, walked everyday in the dark woods, and only left the mountains once, when she took a bus to the coast. There she went to a marine junk shop, where she bought a set of shark jaws filled with the meanest-looking teeth you ever saw. Matilda brought them back and put them on her mantelpiece, next to a strange-looking rattle of bone and wood that she had carved. That rattle sounded, when she shook it, for all the world like something grinding its teeth in Dark Pond.

After just two years of Matilda's mischief, Dark Pond was all but deserted. Fishermen discovered excellent catches elsewhere. Swimmers and campers found better spots.

For a time, Matilda seemed content. There on Dark Pond lived Matilda and a few others, not more than six people on a nine-mile long pond. That should have been enough solitude for anybody.

It was not enough for Matilda. She brooded and brooded about those others still living on "her" pond. No matter what she did nobody budged.

It was only after she had put a torn and bloody human body near the boat landing that Matilda had Dark Pond for herself. No, Matilda hadn't killed anybody. She'd heard the shriek of brakes and run out to the road, where she found a car, badly wrecked. From that car she stole a body. Then she used her shark's teeth on it. She told herself that it didn't matter. It was a car full of strangers and she needed the corpse for a good purpose. It did work. Everyone but Matilda moved away from Dark Pond. And for a while Matilda was happy. She was certain that finally she had Dark Pond all to herself.

Every day Matilda swam in Dark Pond. Every day something swam near her, something that brushed her legs, something that grew each day just a little bit bigger.

Matilda should have known the pond wasn't hers. She should have run away, but she stayed. When the something got big enough, it ate the light from Dark Pond. Matilda saw it. She saw that neither sun, nor moon, nor stars, nor lamp held above the water, no light at all, was reflected in Dark Pond.

But Matilda, stubborn Matilda, stayed. And when the something got big enough, it ate most of Matilda.

The Notebook

*U*sually Gram enjoyed Danny's questions and his interest in her cooking. It was all so normal to have him hanging around the kitchen. Nothing prepared her.

"What's that you're stirring?" Danny stuck in his fingers. "That's awful! I need *lemonade*! Quick!"

Filling his glass, Gram pretended to glare at him. She stirred the batter quickly. "It's a kind of biscuit."

Danny sighed, as if he'd long ago explained something very simple. "Why don't you just cook the regular stuff?"

"Sometimes the new inventions are good," Gram replied, scraping the last of the mixture out of the bowl and beginning to knead it.

Danny grinned, then abruptly became very offhand. "Gram." He poured himself more lemonade. "I wanted to ask you if you know any stories with no endings?"

"Can't think of any. Why?"

"Like you go to listen to all those storytellers over to the Grange and all. Are there any stories that were started and never finished?"

"Nope. Those storytellers have endings, else folks wouldn't go." He nodded. "Movies, books, all of them;

you may not like the ending, but . . . only dreams just leave off."

Danny picked at the flour on the edges of the dough. "Second taste of this stuff ain't half bad."

"Hummph." The old lady kneaded twice more, gently. Then she asked, "Been dreaming again?"

"No. Just wondering." With a crash of the screen door, the boy went outside, then returned. "What's for dinner?"

"Chicken, biscuits, corn, gravy, some wilted lettuce if you'll pick it later."

"Sure."

Once the boy was out of sight, the old lady cleaned her hands. He had been dreaming again. What could she do?

With one last look out the screen door, she left the kitchen. Just inside the parlor, she stopped for a minute. Once her eyes had adjusted to the dim light within the room, she hurried over to a big old roll-top desk. All its pigeonholes overflowed with papers, pencils, tapes, and string. Ignoring them, she reached into her dress and unpinned a small key, with which she opened the largest drawer in the desk. From the drawer she took a thick, untidy notebook. Her hands trembled.

"Now I've taken you out. What'll I do with you?" she muttered. "Drat that boy. There's nothing he can't open if he has a mind to it." Sighing, she sat down to look at the notebook, at first without opening it. Then, slowly, she turned the pages, not even trying to read what was written there.

Eleven years ago that lost girl had come. Gram and Herb had found her by the side of the road. Pushed from a car by the look of it. All beaten up, flaming red hair, pretty, but so dirty, and a face that looked forever lost. Pregnant, said she had no parents. Way she talked, she wasn't from Nebraska. She'd settled in. They had looked for her folks, sent fingerprints to the FBI, but she was of age and no one seemed to be missing her. How could no one miss her? Gram never got over that one. She'd stayed, had her baby and named him Danny. She'd seemed to love him. Gram had taught her how to care for him, and the red-haired girl had done a pretty good job. She was best at keeping the baby clean, but very timid about soothing.

"Oh, he's crying!" she'd wail. "What'll I do?"

"Pick him up." Gram's reply had always been the same.

When was it the girl had started writing in the notebook? Seemed a good thing to do, get her ordered in her mind, record Danny's growth. She wrote every day, a line or so at first, then pages. Then time was Gram would have to look for her. No one would have believed it. Herb still didn't. But then Gram had actually seen it, seen that girl come out of the notebook, looking all lost, come back into the room to hug Danny. But it wasn't good. Each time the girl wrote or read herself into that notebook, she came back to them weaker, paler than she'd been the time before. Gram had begged her to put away the notebook.

Then one day she didn't come out.

"She's run away," insisted Herb.

"No, she hasn't! I saw her in there, with my own eyes, not five minutes ago, even less. Herb, I saw her go into that notebook."

"You didn't."

"I did."

Gram shook away the memory, closed the notebook, smoothed the cover. "What if Danny goes in," she demanded of the untidy bundle of papers, "goes in trying to find an end for whatever dream he's having? Oh, girl, did you send him dreams so he'll come in, or so he'll get you out? Oh, I wish I knew what to do."

She stood up, then sat back down again.

"Where can I put this cursed thing? Back in here or under my mattress?"

Muttering that way, she didn't hear Danny at the doorway, and she jumped when he spoke.

"What's that? Is it a story my mom wrote? Could I read it, Gram? I could. I read good enough."

"Danny. Please. You scared the living daylights out of me. No. It's not your mom's, nothing to do with her, just some old papers, recipes. But I'm not about to cook anything else. Those biscuits are my one failure for today. Did you get that lettuce?"

Danny made no move to leave the room.

"Go! Go! Go! Wash your hands!" Gram ordered.

"Gotta help Gramps first. I'm going!" Danny dragged himself out the door.

Rising quickly, Gram put the notebook back in the

drawer, locked it, and returned the key to its place inside her dress.

"Hopeless," said Herb later that night. "Why did you lie to him?"

"I don't know."

"He's bound to read it. Why didn't you burn the damned thing years ago?"

"I couldn't. I know she's in there. What if she wants to come back? I thought of putting it in the bank vault, but what if she starved there?"

"It's better that she'd have to bust my desk apart before she could get out of that locked drawer?" Herb grinned. "Come on, old lady. Let's sleep. Us old farmers got to get up mornings."

"How'm I going to make sure he don't read it?"

"Give it to him for homework," said Herb, pretending to snore. Herb was right, as usual. For the next three days, Gram moved the notebook around the house like a young cat with its first litter. No place was good enough, and her preoccupation made Danny particularly attentive. Consequently, Gram was almost relieved when she found Danny on his bed, turning the pages of the notebook. He was reading. He looked safe. He might learn something about his mother that would help him; he might not.

Gram's time of hiding the notebook, of worrying whether she was supposed to save it or destroy it, that time was over.

One thing alone had not ended: her fear. Gram didn't

say a word. Down she went to the kitchen, her refuge, and began to bake everything Danny liked best to eat, as if food and love could keep him safe.

By suppertime Danny was gone.

Herb sat across the table from her. Three plates were set. Two plates had food, untouched, on them. The third plate was clean.

"What should we do? You saw him go into the notebook?"

Herb nodded. "I saw."

She sighed. "We've lost him."

"No. Danny isn't lost, never has been. He'll come out."

"You sure? And won't it tempt him, and he'll go back, and each time he does he'll get weaker and weaker until he don't return to us—just like his mother?" She was crying.

"No," said Herb, "I'm not sure, but I think Danny likes being alive."

The next day Gram did not ask Herb about sure, or even maybe.

The day after that, she made no meals. Herb, without a word, fixed breakfast for them both after he had cared for the animals. Gram knew he was worried, though he'd never come out and say it. All day she sat in her kitchen chair, not moving. Herb came back at noon. He touched her shoulder lightly, then left the kitchen.

"Danny!" He called up the stairs to the boy's room, "Chores to be done. I'm too old to take care of the cows alone!"

"Herb, how could you make fun of me?"

"I'm not; it just occurred to me, maybe we could call him back. It's worth a try. Here, have some coffee. What are these, biscuits?"

"A failure. Danny said they tasted awful."

"Not so bad." He put another in his pocket and went back to work.

She was asleep, a cup of cold coffee in front of her on the kitchen table, when someone touched her hand.

"Gram?"

"Danny, Danny!"

"I heard Gramps calling me. It scared me to see you asleep like that. Isn't supper ready yet? I'm starving. I'll even eat these failure biscuits. Hey!" He stopped. "Why are you crying?"

"You have been gone inside that notebook for three entire days. Your grampa and I have been worried sick." Her voice shook so that she couldn't even pretend to be calm the way she'd want to be.

"Three days? And I hurried. I'm so hungry. Gramps! I was just coming to help you. I heard you call me."

"Want to tell us what's in there?" Herb managed a conversational tone, but his hand was shaking when he poured three cups of coffee, filled one with milk and slid it over to Danny's place. "It's like a dream, pieces of dreams, and lost people. Sad mostly. I just kept walking and walking, never seeing anyone I knew. I did know the way out, really, I just lost track of the time. When Gramps called, I offered to lead some people out, but they wouldn't come." Danny hugged both his grandparents. "I'm sorry it was so long, really!"

"It's okay, but there's no supper yet, just leftovers."

"And these." Herb handed Danny the last biscuit. "That's okay. It's all okay."

"What are we going to do with the notebook?"

"I don't care." Danny's mouth was full. "Throw it away, burn it. I won't read it again."

He was quiet for a moment. "No, maybe not; put it away. Maybe I'll think of an ending for it someday."

How I Kill
My Stepmothers

*Y*ou *probably* know my father, everyone does. He's fabulously wealthy even for a count, but he loves to work in his gardens. You can find him there most of the time, grubbing about his plants. He's famous. He has both trees and flowers named for him.

You may have known my mother. She was lovely, but she died when we were very young. We, my sisters and I, are fair, golden, as she was. My father knows it well.

For a long time after our mother died my father was sad, but then something even more dreadful happened. He was bewitched. My father brought home a new wife. She was our first stepmother. For two days we watched, my sisters and I, while wagons brought the dowry of our new stepmother to our beautiful home. The servants carried it past us: linens, clothes, paintings, silver, jewels. Then it all had to be put away, put away in our own beloved rooms, with Father's little wife directing them all. It was days before my sisters and I could begin our work on her. Foolish woman! She thought because we were children she could win us to her. We taught her!

The very first time that Father left us alone with her while he went to his gardens, we began. It was in the sun-bright breakfast room that we waited for her. By saying that we would care for our new stepmother, we had persuaded the servants to leave us alone with her.

She arrived, wishing us good morning. Before she could do more, we began.

"You!" said my sister. "Those are my mother's pearls you wear. How dare you defile them!"

"You!" said my other sister. "That is my mother's gown you wear. How dare you defile it!"

"You!" I cried. "This is our mother's house. The very air you breathe is not yours! Get out!"

Through it all our stepmother could only whisper, "No, no, no." Although she could bewitch our father, she had no power over us. She was young and weak. We were younger and stronger. No one ever heard us. No one saw. Father's second wife never told a living soul. When Father was present, we ignored her. When alone with her, we gave her no rest.

And so we defeated her.

Father thought it was the baby she carried inside her that killed her, that killed them both. But we knew, my sisters and I. My sisters were loyal then.

For years life went on quite pleasantly. My sisters and I were our father's golden rays of sunshine. We could do everything just the way our dear mother would have done it. Then, without warning, Father brought a "special" guest for dinner, the Lady Ilona, a widow with married sons. Father told us at that dinner, told us that he and the Lady Ilona intended to wed. Ilona. Lady Ilona with her insufferable calm. Ilona of the red-brown hair and long hands that touch everything.

This time my weakling sisters fell. Oh, the relieved look on Father's face as they became friends with the Lady Ilona. Oh, the patience on my father's face as he tried not to notice my loathing for this intruder.

No word, no accusation, no look could mar her calm. She offered to teach me! She smiled and turned her back when I told her she must leave.

Nothing worked to rid us of this woman, my stepmother, until I called up the dark spirits.

I have used every means of magic I could muster. Now, at last a spirit has come to help me. I shall succeed, though at first the spirit alarmed me. I thought it looked far too much like my first stepmother to please me. But the spirit's counsel is sound, and I am following it. To bring about the horrible, slow, and painful death of my stepmother, the Lady Ilona, I have completely removed myself from the family, to a room in the corner of the house farthest from the sight or sound of anyone. Here have I closed myself inside, to make magic both day and night. Here, sitting on my heels, arms wrapped around my knees, I concentrate my growing power.

I answer no summons. I admit no living person to my room. I need neither food nor drink. I am all power.

Soon, soon . . .

Tim the Alien

*O*ne *day* a boy named Tim, who liked everything about rockets and crumbly cookies, walked to the grocery store with twenty-five cents in his pocket. Tim had found that quarter glittering in the grass in front of his house the minute he went out the door that morning. Tim was hungry, so he set out to see what the twenty-five cents would buy.

Inside the grocery store, all the cookies Tim saw were too expensive, so he turned around to leave. There, just beside the checkout stand, was a huge box with a large sign on it.

```
                  25¢
       INTRODUCTORY OFFER!!!
         ALIEN COOKIES
```

There was one box of cookies left. Quickly Tim picked up the box of Alien Cookies and paid for it with his quarter. His mouth watering, Tim opened the rocket-shaped cookie box. Inside were yellow-green crumbly alien cookies. Each one had a different shape, each had a friendly, crooked little yellow-green smile. Strange color, thought Tim, but I'll try one anyway. The taste was terrific, so he took another.

Outside the store Tim stood in the warm sunshine, eating his alien cookies. It only took a minute to finish the whole box. Tim sighed. He could have eaten more. Carefully he put the box into his pocket so that he could play with it later. Many people passed Tim while he stood there eating his alien cookies. Not a single person noticed that Tim's arms had become just a little bit yellow and crumbly.

The next morning Tim woke up early. He was all crumbly, a crumbly yellow-green alien from a far planet, and Tim the Alien was very hungry.

Quietly Tim crept up to his big sister's room, where he found a great many books on the floor. The first one he ate said *How to Turn Aliens into Humans*.

Page by page, Tim the Alien ate the book. After that, page by page, he ate his sister's diary and an exciting mystery she had not finished reading.

Just as Tim the Alien was thoughtfully chewing the last page of still another book, his big sister woke up.

"Tim! You rat! You ate everything!" She yelled.

It was not quite true because her room was full of books and Tim was still hungry.

"You!" she screamed. "For this I'll leave you an alien and sell you to the zoo."

She did, too.

It all happened so quickly that Tim wasn't even very mad at his big sister. He merely looked around the zoo, and the zoo animals looked at him.

One by one they came over to him, and sniffed at him, and one by one they nibbled him.

At first Tim was scared and yelled, "Cut that out!"

But what he really said was "Bjfzzzzzt!" in Alien.

The animals kept on nibbling.

With great relief Tim saw that whatever part of yellow-green crumbly Tim they nibbled, it just grew right back, so he stopped being worried.

Also, after nibbling, the animals began to speak to him in Alien. "Bljfzkkkk . . . Welcome. You taste good."

"Thanks," said Tim.

Then Tim and the animals talked things over.

"How do you like it here?" Tim asked.

"It's not so bad," said the lion, "a bit crowded and a bit tedious, but most of us can't go anywhere else."

"Why not?" asked Tim.

"Some of us come from places that are cities now," said the gazelle.

"Some of us were born in zoos," said the leopard.

"Let's," said Tim, "build a spaceship. I'll pilot us to my alien planet. We can live there, and not in a zoo. And we won't even take my big sister."

"Sounds good," agreed all the animals.

"What," asked the giraffe in a whisper, "can we use to build it?"

"What do we have the most of?" asked Tim.

"Peanut shells, stale popcorn, and cage bars," replied the lion, counting them off on his claws.

Tim set to work designing.

Within days, Tim, the gorillas, the monkeys, and the elephants were building the spaceship frame, using every other cage bar. That way no one would notice the missing bars.

The rest of the animals chewed up peanut shells and stale popcorn, which tasted simply dreadful, and spat them into a huge trough. To that mixture, Tim added some crumbly yellow-green Tim toes (which then grew right back). The mixture frothed and foamed, forming a wonderful material. "Great!" cried Tim. "This is our outer shell and spacecraft solar power system. It will take over after we achieve blast-off."

The elephants sprayed that mixture on the frame of the spaceship to make the hull.

They worked hard, and hid the project so cleverly that they were sure no one suspected. Not even Tim's big sister, who came every day to say she was sorry for selling Tim to the zoo. Although he was no longer angry with her, Tim was working so hard that he didn't even say "zzzkkfttz," so Tim's sister went back home.

In no time at all Tim the Alien and the animals had built a fine spaceship, filled it with provisions, and prepared to depart. One gloomy night Tim sat up late, working on the final arrangements for the spaceship blast-off fuel system.

Bad luck! Tim and the animals had not noticed one important thing. Someone had seen them.

Mean Mr. McFoo, who usually took away the peanut shells and stale popcorn from the zoo, had discovered their secret project. McFoo was furious at Tim and the animals because he had always used the peanut shells and stale popcorn as filling for the shoddy little stuffed animals he sold outside the main gate of the zoo. He wanted those shells back, and he wanted the animals and Tim to stay right there in the zoo so that McFoo's business would go on as usual.

Late that night, Mean Mr. McFoo sneaked up to where Tim nodded, half asleep, over his plans for the fuel system.

With the flame from his powerful cigar and brier-pipe lighter, McFoo set fire to the straw that covered the cage floor at the bottom of the spaceship.

"Quick! Tim! Fire!!!!" shouted Tim's big sister, who was there once again, hoping Tim would forgive her and come home.

Tim jumped up, wide awake, and called the others.

"Inside the ship! This will be blast-off!"

All the animals came running as fast as they could and quickly clambered aboard.

"Bluoooot," grinned Tim at his sister as she clambered aboard. He offered her a piece of elbow to nibble.

"Xzzzjjjjt," she replied.

Mr. Randolph

*M*r. *Randolph's* tyranny was democratic. His sarcasm slashed them all: girls, boys, the silent shy ones, the brilliant, the big shots. No one escaped.

Everyone knew him, a tall, gaunt man with big yellow teeth and an Adam's apple huge and always moving. Some ghastly vanity made him comb the long, thin strands of his red hair over the bald spot that was the chief ornament of his large head. Perhaps someone, somewhere, had once noticed that his eyes were beautiful, dark blue and very deep. His victims in the school did not.

"That is your answer? Now just what is it in your little pea brain that prompts you to give us precisely that answer today? Pray do tell us."

If it was not your turn, you watched, the way a field mouse watches the snake about to devour it, and you too forgot whether the answer given was the correct one or not. Mr. Randolph attacked correct as well as incorrect answers.

"Correct? The answer you gave ten weary minutes ago, before I was forced to give the proof, was correct? Well then, my dear, dear liberated female"—for boys it might be "my sweet pimply adolescent"—"why did you lack the courage of your convictions? Hmmmmm? Perhaps we can continue?"

Anything could set him off. Even failing to respond with "Mr. Randolph, sir" could bring down a sarcastic tirade.

Mr. Randolph never lacked for words, or for energy. With parents and the powerful ones in the school system he was, quite simply, charming. He never fawned, instead he was all Virginia charm, slightly courtly.

Stories went around the school that some tragedy had happened to make him hate the kids so much, but no one knew for sure. Another persistent rumor over the years was that the other teachers weren't fooled by his charm with adults, and some parents had tried to ease Randolph out of teaching. They had failed.

Randolph ate little and drank even less. The man seemed to have no weak spots. Year after year kids passed through his classes, suffering, hating him, without a sliver of justice to sweeten their lives.

And so Mr. Randolph remained triumphant until the November night when flu struck down three of the people with whom he was to have played his weekly game of bridge. His usual response to the missed evening of cards would have been to look out at the cold rain beating against his windows, and then to take a good book down from the shelf and read. But on that November night Mr. Randolph went out. He drove the dark, wet roads to another town, where he found a bar, a dull place with loud music and a television set, the whole of it thick with smoke. There he remained long, long past his normal bedtime, until smoke, fatigue, and the drink he had consumed made him yearn for sleep.

From the bar Mr. Randolph walked out into the raw, cold night, to the parking lot where he had left his car. Once in the driver's seat, he closed the car door, started the engine, then sat until the motor ran smoothly. He was so very tired, his head ever so slightly abuzz. Mr. Randolph rolled down the window next to him. He'd need that cold air to stay awake.

With intense concentration, he carefully drove his gray sedan homeward, home to bed and sleep. Mr. Randolph's care was insufficient, however, because it was not very long before he saw the flashing red lights of a police car in his rearview mirror. Obediently he pulled his car to the side of the road and stopped.

"Good evening, sir. May I see your driver's license and registration?"

Mr. Randolph found the papers without too much difficulty. The trooper looked long at the license and at Mr. Randolph, whose only thought was of his bed, of sleep.

"Please," said the trooper, "step out of your car and walk here by the side of the road."

Obediently Mr. Randolph followed the trooper's instructions, walking with all the dignity he could muster.

"Easy there," said the trooper, reaching out a steady hand. . . . But before he could continue, they both heard the shrill screech of tires on wet pavement, horns honking, a silence, one crash, then another, followed by a still greater silence. Mesmerized, Mr. Randolph watched the young trooper turn, run to pick up his car radio, speak into it rapidly, and return it to its place. Then, smoothly, the trooper ran toward the accident, across the broad meadow that separated the road on which Mr. Randolph stood from the highway on the other side. Over his shoulder the young trooper ordered, "Stay right there and wait for me!"

Mr. Randolph waited, rain pelting his face. How long he waited, he had no idea. His only thought was of his bed, of how it would be to lie down, to ease his bones, to stretch his full length onto his bed and sleep.

With a jerk, Mr. Randolph was awake. He'd dozed off while leaning against the wet car. Momentarily alert now, Mr. Randolph was more himself, the man in command. Surely he did not have to wait any longer. Surely that young trooper had forgotten completely what he had been doing.

Into the car went Mr. Randolph, started the engine, and drove, always carefully, home. Into the narrow street on which he lived, he turned the car, down the row of tall, narrow houses to the very last one, home.

Odd, the garage door was open. He'd never been so careless before. Mr. Randolph parked the car. Sleepy, he got out, went to the kitchen door and pushed the button to close the garage door. The kitchen door, protected as it normally was by the locked garage door, was always open. Mr. Randolph hated to lock himself out merely because he had gone to fetch something stored in the garage. Inside, Mr. Randolph passed through the kitchen into the hall. There he deposited his keys on the hall table. He threw his dripping raincoat over the bannister and went upstairs. He dropped his clothes onto a straight-backed chair, then went into the bathroom, brushed his teeth, and took two aspirin.

Finally Mr. Randolph slid his tired body into the bed; if only it would not move before he slept.

Mr. Randolph did sleep, deeply. It took many long rings of the doorbell to rouse him, several hours later. It was still quite dark.

Sleepily, Mr. Randolph found his robe. He managed first one hand, and then the other, into the sleeves. Tying the sash badly, he went downstairs to the front door. Through the glass panels alongside it he could see who stood there: silhouettes of two state troopers on the front step, a black and white police car parked at the curb behind them.

He opened the door.

"Good morning, Mr. Randolph. Could you tell us, were you stopped by a state trooper early this morning, on Doppler Road, and asked to remain on the scene?"

Mr. Randolph never hesitated. "I? No. I have been asleep for hours."

"And your car, is it in the garage? May we see it?"

Mr. Randolph shrugged. "See it? Certainly."

One of the troopers sent the garage door up, effortlessly. There, before the open door, they stood, Mr. Randolph, tall and scrawny in his frayed robe, and the two young giants. The three of them stood beneath that single streetlight in the November rain that seemed never to stop.

And Mr. Randolph looked into his garage. The car inside was a shining black and white police car, the twin of the one parked in the quiet street behind them. For one stunned second Mr. Randolph sagged, then he smoothed his thin hair and smiled his big yellow-toothed smile, all Virginia charm.

But the young trooper cut him off. "Don't even bother. We've waited a long time, Mr. Randolph—sir."

Hookman

". . . for better or worse, till death do us part."

No one saw any strangers at the wedding, when Jeff and Carole were married in the little green Episcopal church high up on Church Street. It was Carole's church, and Jeff agreed, though he was from Vermontville and not Anglican at all.

Carole was a pretty, fluffy blonde, and a darned good hairdresser; everyone said so. She and Jeff had known each other since high school, though at first she had dated Ben, Jeff's best friend. After Carole and Ben broke up (Jeff never asked why), Jeff had waited a long time before he asked Ben, would he mind if Jeff asked Carole out. Ben had shrugged. "Go ahead, why not?"

And now, years later, Jeff and Carole were getting married, and Ben was best man. Granny had shaken her head at that news. "Ask your brother instead. It's bad luck to ask Ben after he lost her." But Jeff laughed. "Oh Granny, you don't understand. That was years ago. Ben's my best friend."

"No," Granny had replied. "It's you who doesn't understand. Wedding's a fragile thing. Ben's not glad, 'n' hate lets evil in."

But Jeff had kept insisting, and Jeff was her favorite,

so Granny did attend the wedding, but she refused even to set foot in the reception. Jeff's folks left early to take her home. Still, it was a cheerful wedding, with all the pickups lined up in front of the church, shining, decorated with flowers and bright crepe-paper streamers.

It was a fall wedding, with the girls in taffeta dresses, guys in formals. Only Ben had forgotten his shoes, so he wore sneakers instead, which made them all laugh. Ben too.

Then the reception. Aunt Rhea, who is silly, kissed Carole and Jeff too many times, getting them wet with her tears. She's the one who painted a porcelain platter for their wedding present. She couldn't decide whether to do it with cupids or strawberries all over, so she did both.

Silly Aunt Rhea sobbed, "Honeys, this is the *first* day of the rest of your lives!" Ben rolled his eyes behind her back, and one bridesmaid giggled, hoping he'd notice her.

But then, when it was too late to send someone to get the darned thing, it turned out that Ben had also forgotten Jeff's suitcase from home. Carole and Jeff would have to drive clear to Jeff's for the suitcase, which contained all Jeff's clothes for their honeymoon trip. Only then could they begin the two-hour drive out of the mountains up to Montreal for their honeymoon. "A city trip for a mountain girl," Jeff had promised.

"Ben's sure been a mess-up today," someone complained. "At least he didn't lose the ring," said Aunt Minerva.

"Oh! I'd have given you mine!" cried Uncle Oscar. Everyone laughed.

None of it mattered to Carole and Jeff. This was a day nothing could spoil.

While the dancing was in full swing, Carole slipped away from the reception to dress for the city, in a pretty suit and pretty high-heeled shoes that were mostly straps. Jeff helped her up into the truck and they left Saranac Lake, streamers billowing out behind them.

The wind picked up, and the night got cold before they were out of town. Dark came early in the forest village; houses were closed up, fires going. They drove and drove, past old Farleigh, who shut his doors and windows at dark and never opened them till light. He was a man afraid of the dark, of the wind, of the forest pressing around him.

Carole moved closer to Jeff, shivering. The yellow headlights picked out a narrow path of road ahead, forest all around. Then they turned left, down the long road to Jeff's house.

Darn Ben. Because he'd forgotten the suitcase, they'd lose more than an hour by the time they got back to the highway, and Carole was thinking how she hated night driving, fearing the deer that would leap out and crash into them, fearing not seeing beyond the yellow path of their own headlights, and hating the high beams of oncoming cars that blinded her watchfulness. Jeff hugged her. "Could sleep at my house, but I kinda hate to waste our Montreal fancy hotel room."

Carole kissed his cheek. "It's okay. We can sleep late tomorrow."

Abruptly, the engine sputtered, then died.

"That's never happened before," said Jeff. They coasted to a stop. Jeff tried to start the engine, and failed.

"Can't work on it dressed in these rented clothes. Let's walk the rest of the way home, and I'll change, get my dad's car." He held her close, then felt the cloth of her sleeves. "Hey, that jacket's kinda thin. You'd best wait at home where it's warm."

Carole groaned and pointed to her feet. "The jacket's not the problem. I have my coat. It's these."

"Oh," said Jeff, "you can't walk far or fast in those."

"No, I can't. Here I've spent my whole life in sneakers and boots, and now look. I don't have anything but silly city shoes in my suitcase. This was going to be a city trip."

"Look," said Jeff. "You stay here, bundle up in your coat. I'll run home, run the whole way. Okay?"

"Sure. I'm not scared."

Jeff closed the door and was gone in the darkness. After a second's hesitation, Carole locked both doors. She wanted to laugh at herself. She'd never been scared; she grew up here. These forests were home, but the wind blew round the edges of the truck, and the night was without light from stars or moon. It seemed she'd been waiting forever. As the wind grew stronger, the trees leaned toward the truck, closer and closer. Their branches scraped the truck cab, and Carole was sure she felt the truck tremble. As if someone climbed up on it. Tremble and pull. Was someone pulling at the door? I can't be scared. It must be my imagination, thought Carole; her hands, unsteady, grasped the steering wheel. Tremble. Was the cab shaking? Or was she?

Carole groped for the ignition key. Maybe it would start now. Maybe it had just been some dirt or something in the fuel line. Tremble.

She tried the engine, afraid to look at the windows to her right or left, not sure what she saw out of the corner of her eye. The engine started, died. Easy now, give it more gas, not too much; try again. Started! Slamming the brake release, Carole gave the truck gas. It lurched forward. She gave it more gas. Tires spinning gravel from the roadside, the truck leaped ahead. Carole turned on the headlights, gave the truck gas down to the floor. Carole drove, drove, drove toward Jeff's house on the narrow, deserted road. Where were the house lights? It was never so far. All about her the wind whipped the branches against the sides of the truck. Carole drove. There's the driveway. With a spray of gravel she pulled in. She was crying. It was so far! Why was she so scared? Everyone looked so surprised to see her. They all talked at once.

"Where's Jeff?"

"No fight yet?"

Laughter.

Then all the faces white around her. Jeff's father going round to the passenger side. Jeff's mother helping Carole down from the driver's side. Carole so scared. *Jeff not there?* Then his father holding something metal.

"What is it?"

"A hook caught in the window."

Everyone gathered around, looking but unwilling to touch it.

"An ice hook?" someone whispered.

The wind stirred the dry leaves around their feet.

Carole insisted she'd ride back to show them the spot. But when they got there Carole closed her eyes not to see what swayed in the wind, above where the truck had been standing, swayed there with shoes shined for a wedding.

Hookman? He lacks neither hooks, nor couples, nor patience, nor evil.

Author's Note

A version of the Hookman story was told to me by my children, who heard it from some teenagers, who in turn had heard it at an Adirondack campfire and down in Tennessee. I have been told that Hookman preys only on newly married couples, but after a Hookman story, not one of my children is willing even to visit the outhouse at night unescorted. The kids also claim that Hookman has plastered-down brown hair and a pencil-thin mustache, and that if you eat enough garlic, he can't get you. But with Hookman, how much is enough?

Dr. Egger's Favorite Dog

I *don't* even like dogs. You may well say, "Of course not; she's an old-maid doctor with nails too short and hands too clean and skin all dried up from too much work, too little sleep, and from bossing people around." Maybe, but I love my sister and her family, her soft-hearted husband, and her six kids. I even love to visit them, though I could never live in their constant tumult.

It was Dan, my sister's soft-hearted husband, who brought that monster puppy home from the lumberyard. It was a gift, he said, from a customer. But I'll bet Dan had saved that pup from drowning, which is the usual way for disposing of extra dogs around here.

They got that pup when Cappy was seven. The dog and the girl grew up together. And I mean together! The farthest from Cappy that pup ever did get was to have his head resting on her foot. By the time Cappy was eleven, the pup was a shaggy black giant, gentle and smart. It was some sort of Newfoundland and Labrador mixture. Not handsome, but big. I called it Dog, as I have always called all dogs.

We're a close family, but I was around a bit more than

usual the winter of the accident, for I had just cut back my practice. It was time to give the young patients and doctors a go at one another. The old folks and I (I'm twenty years older than my sister), well, we old folks stuck together. But as I had some time, I had been driving Cappy around, mostly to visit veterinarians doing farm work. It was Cappy's intention to be a vet; she always had a way with animals.

The weather was the nastiest late winter can offer. There was ice, rain, sleet, and fog coming and going for weeks on end. The best days were merely bleak. Cappy and her classmate Gloria were assigned to write a report together, on coyotes. There aren't too many coyotes in the Adirondacks, but I'd taken them to visit an old friend, a vet who had once done some studies on coyotes. Naturally, Cappy had asked to take the dog with us, in my clean car! So there he sat, as much as possible on Cappy's lap as we drove those mountain roads.

Afterward, I dropped Gloria at her house, which is way out off the highway. Getting home was as unpleasant a piece of driving as you are likely to find anywhere. The immediate forecast was bad, with worse promised to follow. I wasn't pleased when Cappy said she was going home from school with Gloria the next day, to work on their report. I asked her why they couldn't work in town. Well, no, Cappy told me; they couldn't this time because Gloria had to baby-sit for her younger brother and sister.

The following day was horrible. The schools were

closed early to be sure to get the kids home by dark. Cappy, stubborn as a mule, went home with Gloria. She called her mom to say that in the worst case she'd spend the night. Meanwhile Heaven threw down what it could: ice, snow, and rain, and wrapped it all in a killer fog. It was weather not fit for man or beast. I was thinking about closing my office and heading on home when my sister telephoned. She was upset. Half an hour earlier the dog had begun to pace and whine. My sister told him to hush, that Cappy wouldn't be home, wasn't even near home. He'd kept it up, acting desperate, so she thought he was sick and needed to get out.

My sister could hardly get the door open. The dog rushed outside. With no hesitation he was gone, into the fog at a dead run.

Now, my sister hasn't a hysterical bone in her body, and she raised five kids before Cappy, so I knew she'd never fret without reason. The dog had long ago learned that Cappy went alone to school and that Cappy visited friends. "If," my sister said, "Cappy is safe at Gloria's, as bad as the storm is, the dog should not be so upset, should not run off like that. If he's gone to fetch Cappy, something must be wrong!" She'd tried to call Gloria's house but the lines were down. She'd had no better luck trying to reach Dan. I told her not to drive out looking for Cappy, but to wait and stay off the telephone so that she could receive calls. I'd do the telephoning.

One telephone call did get through, the one from the hospital. Cappy was there. She'd been hit by a logging truck that bucked and twisted in the ice and fog. Cappy was there, unconscious. She was so thin and so quiet she hardly made a bump in the bed.

I went to the hospital and stayed there with her, as aunt, not as doctor. I sat and waited, asking with everything I had that Cappy not slip into the coma that is living death. We took turns that night, my sister, Dan, and I, and during my time alone with Cappy I sat wondering what had made her go out to the highway and walk there where no one could see her, especially not a truck out of control on the ice.

It was well after midnight when the dog came. Suddenly, there he was, outside the ground-floor window of Cappy's room, standing with his nose on the glass. I opened the window, wondering how I'd drag that great bulk over the sill, but he leaped over it as if it were no higher than a blade of grass.

Yes, I let him in, wet, dirty dog or no. I'd have tried anything to bring Cappy out, to bring her back to us. To my relief, he did not shake out his dripping fur. Without hesitation he went to stand by Cappy's side. Softly he whimpered to her.

I saw no change. The dog, too, must have been desperate, for he put his head on the bed, touched her hand. I held my own breath, waiting. No change.

Whimpering insistently, he pushed his great wet black nose under her hand. No change. He whined, louder. Oh dog, I thought, don't bark at her. Instead, his pink tongue went around her motionless hand. Cappy's closed eyes moved, as they do when one dreams. Her fingers twitched, closed gently on the dog's muzzle. Slowly her hand slid up his head, rested, then stroked it, first feebly, then with more strength. The dog stayed, no longer insisting.

I waited. Cappy opened her eyes. Her pupils focused. She saw me, saw the dog, smiled. I waited. "Well, McDuff," said I, calling the dog by his name for the first time ever. "You are a fine friend. I forgive you all your doggy ways: the dirt, the fur everywhere, the constant need to go in or out, being underfoot. I even forgive that doggy look that asks, 'What wonderful thing are we going to do now?'" I touched his back, which he bore patiently. He didn't look at me, only at Cappy.

After a while Cappy cautiously moved her legs and wriggled her toes. Then, satisfied that they still worked, she slept. It was genuine sleep, her breathing regular, the sleep she needed to heal her. I must have dozed, for Cappy woke me up. The dog was gone. Cappy was teasing me for letting the dog into the hospital. I muttered something about never living it down because whoever had put him out of her room would certainly tell everybody in the whole hospital. I knew I'd spend the rest of my life explaining my having let him in.

While I looked after her, Cappy told me how, while she was at Gloria's, there had been a fight. Gloria and her father had screamed at one another in a kind of fury Cappy had never even imagined. It scared her; she couldn't stand to see something so awful, so private. Cappy could not bear to shame her classmate so by witnessing it.

Desperate to get away, Cappy had put on her jacket

and boots and left the house. She intended to walk home, thinking not of the weather but only of the twisted faces and ugly words that filled the house behind her. The dog had found her on the road. Surely he had run the whole way to meet her.

In his doggy mind he must have sensed the fear that made Cappy run away. Did he know she was in danger? In the fog, Cappy did not see the truck until it hit.

Afterward the others came to the hospital, and I got ready to go, intending to give the dog the biggest steak, or slab of liver, and a bone to last a week or more. I asked my sister whether the dog was at home or outside waiting.

As I spoke my sister shook her head at me, whispering, "No, no, no." At last she pulled me out into the corridor and said, to me alone, "Don't. Please don't mention the dog. It's too soon to tell Cappy."

My sister was frantic, but I was blank.

"Too soon to tell Cappy what?"

"Don't you see? The dog is dead. He was between Cappy and the truck. He was killed the minute it struck. He saved her. The people who found them tossed his body over the cliff, into the lake where the ice is mostly gone. . ."

I hugged my sister.

"I'd have buried him for Cappy's sake," she said.

"Don't worry," I whispered, "Cappy will understand."

Flawless Beauty

*T*ime to sleep.

Tara is in Athens now, on her way, according to the newspapers, to an auction somewhere in the Middle East. I had hoped to see her one last time before I die. There was a question I was longing to ask.

Girls like Tara always have someone like me tagging along behind them. That someone is always male, not through fear of competition; no, definitely not. For Tara, I was always there, the quieter, younger, somewhat poorer cousin, slavish, she supposed, in my devotion.

"Ah, cousin Bruno," she'd say. "Put down your book. Let's do something amusing."

Our paths did diverge, mine into my studies, hers into the life of the society beauty. She visited, of course, and I listened, as I had always done. I knew the family history. I could be counted on to appreciate her triumphs.

At one such visit, she announced, "Bruno. I've no longer earmarked a large sum to be used for plastic surgery once I start to become less beautiful."

I choked on the black paste she declared was the

finest of coffee. "Plastic surgery? You are twenty years old! Such things are decades away for someone as stunning as you."

"Yes, yes, dear Bruno, but even so, plastic surgery would be too late. I have looked carefully at all the repaired old beauties. Their faces are dead, good only for a camera held rather far away, to say nothing of the body and the spirit of life. No, no. I have discovered something for me alone. Bruno, you'll be proud of me. I have done research!"

"What are you babbling about?" I stirred some milk into the sludge that remained in my cup.

"At an otherwise tedious dinner in a musty little castle in Mudestellenhof, I learned of a collection of ancient glass bottles once owned by Suleiman I, though the bottle in question is far more ancient, of course."

"I didn't know you were interested in old glass!" The girl could surprise me, after all.

"I'm not, you dolt! One of those bottles still has a genie in it, a rather powerful one I am told. Finally, after a great deal of work, all done by me alone, I have found that bottle, and I have bought it, though of course no one knows why. I've kept it all secret, for if I have even a whim, all those society hangers-on immediately rush to copy it." She giggled, shaking her hair. I looked at Tara, at those blue eyes, that shimmering hair, that flawless skin, at her movements languidly fluid.

"Pure form, pure beauty," I muttered, "with no content. Not a brain in your head. Genie indeed."

"No, no, Bruno. Indulge me. Come with me. My treat."

I went.

The bottle was to be delivered to her in Beirut, and we had to go there. I never understood why.

Through the rubble, through those wretched streets, Tara led me, though I could barely walk.

"What, Bruno afraid?" Tara thought to taunt me into making more speed.

"No. It's not fear."

She gave me a sharp look. "Ahh yes. I remember now. You knew Beirut once as a boy, didn't you?" Her voice softened. "It was nice, wasn't it?"

I could not help but sigh. Tara the trivial. "Yes," I said, "nice."

Her bottle was in a dark basement, more ruin than shop. Once he had placed the bottle in Tara's hands, the proprietor simply backed away from us into the shadows and was gone.

I stood, waiting, thinking how she'd take it when there was no genie, no magic. I thought how I'd pick up the pieces of my beautiful cousin and take her home. Funny, I had always thought she was too stupid, and far too self-centered to ever go mad. But then madness would indeed protect her from age. Among these thoughts I heard, as I often have, the voice of our grandmama saying "You don't choose your family." I was there with Tara, as the good dutiful cousin, and I'd take care of Tara.

Moistening her lips with the tip of her tongue, Tara held the bottle in those slender, well-manicured hands. Carefully, she tested the stopper of the bottle. With a little screech, it moved.

"Bruno, here goes. I'll miss you when you are old and when you are gone, but I am going to have such fun!"

Out came the stopper.

Above us, around us, overpowering us was something. It spoke with a voice that penetrated my very bones, making me tremble then as I tremble now to recall it. My mind, however, was clear, perhaps the clearest it's ever been.

"Mistress. You have summoned me."

"I have," said Tara, as composed as if she, the perfect society beauty, were about to order tea. "I command you to keep me as beautiful as I am at this moment, eternally. Youth," she sighed, "and beauty forever."

"Mistress," asked the voice, "are you to be ageless and beautiful? That and no other is the command you give?"

"That is my command."

"And if it takes away your immortal soul?"

"I have not noticed my immortal soul until now," replied Tara, obviously annoyed at the introduction of the subject.

"And for the rest of humankind? It remains your command?" asked the voice.

"Yes. Everyone enjoys beauty." Tara was firm.

"So be it," replied the voice, and the genie was gone in an explosion that left me choking.

For a moment my burning eyes were closed, then blinded with tears caused by the smoke. I called to Tara once because it was suddenly so terribly silent in that basement.

When I did look, I was alone.

Then, for the first and perhaps the last time, I thought, Poor Tara. Demented by disappointment, had she run away? It was so dark down there. She never could have gotten out.

In my pocket I had a small flashlight. Tara always teased that I was, like the Boy Scouts of old, always prepared. Turning on the light, I looked around the room. There, on the floor, was the genie's bottle, shattered. Beside it lay the stopper, and something else.

All alone in that basement I had to laugh. The wish had come true. Tara was ageless, and a flawless beauty: she was a perfect blue-white diamond of considerable but not vulgar size.

At that moment I faced my own temptations. Should I sell the diamond and make poor, bookish cousin Bruno rich? Should I press it instead into the hand of the first hungry child I met outside that rubble-filled basement room?

I was, I must admit, influenced by that talk of immortal souls, and I had my own sense of our family history. And so, I pocketed Tara, carried her to New York, and gave her to the public library. The sale of the diamond called Tara raised millions of dollars for books, Tara who never read.

I followed her subsequent career. She was sold on numerous occasions, each time for a substantially more staggering sum, and each time the money went for some altruistic cause. Tara the benefactor. Yes, it is a lovely, romantic name for a perfect gem.

Now I am old and dying. I had wanted, longed, to ask Tara if she is pleased at her bargain.

My wants are modest. Perhaps that's why so many of them have been satisfied.

I am awake.

Tara came to me just now, in a dream. She was, as always, quite definite. "Dear Bruno," she said, sitting on the edge of my bed. "You are wondering if I am content. I am. I am. Never, never will I be as you are, rotting flesh waiting for death. No. No. What is more, when the women who wear me begin to see themselves as old, they sell me, quick! I am content."

"Ahh," said I in my dream.

"But Bruno, just one question before we part, you to take your immortal soul and I to eternal beauty . . ."

"Yes?"

"Bruno, dear, bookish, moral Bruno. Was the diamond really the genie's solution or yours?"

Nemesis

Hullo. Yes, Nicholas, I can hear you. No. No. Whatever you do, don't come over here! Yes, I know I haven't been to school. Yes. I'll tell you why.

You're probably the only person I can tell.

You know about bodies and anti-bodies, about particles and anti-particles. You know what happens when a body, say a bacteria or a virus sailing along in your bloodstream, about to give you the flu, meets its antibody.

Poof!

Okay, and you know I've seen plenty of particle/anti-particle collisions over at the university accelerator.

Poof!

Wait a sec, Nicholas. I'm shaking so that I can hardly tell you more. You see, I wonder if I was born just for what's happening. But that's crazy. Biology doesn't work that way! Am I a mutant, a catalyst, or has it always happened? What do I mean? Sorry. I'm ahead of myself. But I can't think of anything else these days. Every particle has its anti-particle, every body its antibody. Even the sun has its dark star: Nemesis.

I make you shudder? Nicholas, I make *me* shudder!

Nicholas. I have been observing people body/anti-body collisions!

No. Nicholas. Really. Listen. No. No. Don't come here! Just listen!

About a year ago I was coming out of the library at just about closing time, when a man, a sallow, dirty bum, collapsed right in front of me. I leaned over to ask if I could help him. I was sort of confused, wondering if I should go back inside to ask one of the librarians to call an ambulance, or what. Then I saw the man, I mean really saw him. He was a sickly mirror-image of my father's friend Professor Hemur. I thought it was odd, and then, out of the library came Professor Hemur. He and the bum looked at one another, and . . .

Poof! Both were gone.

No. Nicholas. It was not my overworked imagination. There is more.

Not three months later (remember when Professor Anderson took me to that physics conference in Paris?) I met an elegant lady at a lunch given by the American scientific attaché. That lady was both intelligent and charming, as well as beautiful.

Two days after I got back home, my mom had a visitor, a friend from San Francisco. Then, Nicholas, the recognition and the awful fear took over. My mother's friend was the counterpart of the woman in Paris!

First, I knew what would happen if the two women were to meet. Second, I realized that one's anti-body is not necessarily a social or professional opposite. No, these women matched in some way I could not perceive.

But match they did. Nicholas, what forces drew them both to Hoboken?

Poof!

I know, I know that two data points are not sufficient, but there is more.

I was scared when I recognized the second collision. Yes, I did see it. But I was horrified that I could not help but think that it would be fascinating to study what precisely are the characteristics of our anti-bodies.

Nicholas. Those collisions always occur after I have seen and recognized the body and anti-body. Am I a catalyst? Are there more people like me? Nicholas, I can't leave my room. No. Really. I was in New York City two weeks ago, walking the streets, trying to think. There, in the masses of people on Fifth Avenue, I saw one here, then another there—blocks apart. Not fifteen minutes later I saw them collide!

Poof!

No. Nicholas. You don't understand. On Fifth Avenue those two people I saw, recognized, and then saw collide—Nicholas, they were little kids!

Maybe, just maybe, if I don't recognize the bodies/anti-bodies, they won't collide.

No. No. Nicholas. Don't come over here!

The Sufficient Prayer

*N*ot *long ago* in a faraway land a little girl was born into the wrong family. (Don't worry, such things don't happen here.)

The girl grew up unhappily, despised by her parents, who called her a stupid clumsy wretch and never set her a place with the others at table. The girl cried a good deal, when she lay alone in the darkness, and said she wished she'd never been born. She often prayed to die. (Don't worry, such things don't happen here.)

She did not die, but grew up and left her parents' house and went into the world, where many good things happened to her. She had the right way with flowers, neither too much nor too little, and a good head for business, and thus made her living well in the world.

But the grown woman was haunted by the despair of the little girl and sometimes gave in to it. It was in those black moods that she repeated the prayer: Oh God, please just let me die. (Don't worry, such things don't happen here.)

After some years, the woman met a man who taught her to laugh. They married. Their children were born into the right family and grew with love. But the woman still could not put to rest the child she had been. There were days when her own children quarreled, days when everything she tried seemed to fail. In those times she became angry with herself and blamed herself for everything bad in the world. Then, just as if she were a despised child instead of a grown woman, she whispered again, "Oh God, please just let me die." (Don't worry, such things don't happen here.)

Once her husband chanced to hear her speak this way. "Bite your tongue!" he said, and would not let her turn her face away. "Every prayer has its sufficient number, a number known only to God. You don't want that prayer to be granted, not when you have a family you love, a family that loves you. Ask such a thing and you may receive it when you want it least. Apologize! Call back those prayers!"

The woman dried her eyes. "I promise," she said, "not ever to pray for death again." And she didn't. But that woman was afraid to call back her old prayers, afraid to apologize. It seemed better, she thought, not to remind God. (Don't worry, such things don't happen here.)

Not long ago in a faraway land that woman walked on a beach in the late-afternoon sunshine. Her husband and children had gone back to the house ahead of her, to sort and arrange the shells they'd collected that day.

The woman was watching the water lapping around her ankles when Death gently touched her hand. "Come now. It's time."

"Please. No."

It was cruel, the people on the beach that late afternoon said to one another, how that freak wave came all the way up on the beach and snatched that poor young woman away. Cruel, people said when they saw her family, for Death to carry off a young woman with everything to live for. Cruel.

(Don't worry, such things don't happen here.)

Will

The first time Will went to the willows at night, alone, he was drawn there by a hunger for all of springtime. No food or drink within the house could quiet the restlessness that pulled him out into the gentle twilight. Did he know the spot was enchanted? Surely in that family he must have heard the whispers.

Carefully Will wheeled his bicycle out of the shed and along the path past a low stone wall crowded with peonies. Their scent, when he came out of the house, was faint. As he walked toward the shed, he breathed more and more deeply, trying to get more and more of it, as if their fragrance alone could satisfy his thirst.

Will walked the bicycle carefully past the heavy dark-green foliage thick with creamy blooms, each with four red points at its heart. The outside petals had the barest touch of pink, like the cheeks of a beautiful girl.

"Oh," said his grandmother's friends over their tea-cups every year, "just look at those peonies! You can always tell an old garden."

"Indeed you can." Gray heads always nodded agreement. "Peonies need time. They want to be put in and left undisturbed for fifty years or so. Then you have a show of blooms." They all said it to one another, and they all had masses of peonies at home in their own gardens. The conversation, repeated over coffee or tea in every garden, was one of the rituals in which they expressed their love for things that stayed, and returned, like the peonies, year after year.

And when they said it, Will's uncle always replied sadly, "Admire them now, because it will rain once they are in full bloom." Once again, everyone always nodded agreement. All the family knew the peonies meant more to Uncle than merely a favorite flower.

Every year Uncle built supports for the long slender stems, and every year he watched sadly as the sodden blossoms bowed their heads and, where they touched the earth, turned brown.

But Will wasn't thinking of his uncle's secret sorrow, or of the peonies, when he coasted down the long driveway, away from the huge, silent house, onto the sandy road that led to the stream that was almost a river.

He went to the willows' lush green, and to the soft spring grass beneath them, with a longing he could neither explain nor resist. He'd felt it all afternoon, ever since he and his family had come home from town, past the willows. When the willows appeared ahead of the car, he had been startled by their green, as if he'd never seen them before. He'd laughed at himself, his own thoughts sounding so much like the grown-ups, who had said such things every year for as long as he could remember. Now at last he was on his way.

Will

Will pedaled easily, glad for the spring rains that had left the road packed down hard. By late summer no amount of pushing could force a bicycle through that sand.

At the edge of the willows, he stopped, put down the bicycle, took off his shoes, and left them there.

Walking across the soft grass, he smelled the willows, the stream, and the grass. The restlessness that brought him here was still not quiet. Did he want to swim?

He stopped by the edge of the water, just next to the circle of white stones, his own fire circle. He'd made it with his big brothers and sisters. How many years ago? They were grown now and gone from home, returning only as visitors.

The moon, which had come up gold on the horizon, was silver now, shimmering on the water, grass, and willows. Will pulled a piece of grass and chewed it. It was sweet. Then, as if he were six years old and still thought that what looked good to him, such as a nice green willow leaf, would also look good to a fish, Will cut a willow wand to use for a fishing pole. Trimming the tip, he tasted a small leaf. It was fine. He was about to use a similar one as a lure when he saw a cluster of bright red berries growing by the side of one willow. Odd, he'd never noticed them before. A single berry, threaded on the willow wand, was perfect, far better than a leaf.

Will settled down to fish and dream in that spring moonlight. Abruptly the willow started in his hands.

Will let the wand out as far as he could, then gently,

slowly pulled it in until he could flick the end out of the water and behind him. There, on the grass, flopped a silver fish, quite beautiful and of a respectable size.

Will, feeling even more triumphant than surprised, admired it for a moment before he started up to gather dry wood.

He had gone no more than three steps when someone called to him.

"Please, won't you dance with me?" Will turned. Where only a second ago there had been a fish, a slender girl stood on the moon-silver grass. Will gasped at her beauty. She then laughed in what seemed to Will an embarrassed delight. Will was certain it was because he looked so silly.

"Will you dance with me?" she repeated, reaching out for him.

"Of course." Will took her hands. They were as warm as his own. She was real, so real, with her eyes of willow green. Black hair fell down to her waist. Her dress, of something soft and white, went from her shoulders to her feet, which were bare. Her arms too were bare, her skin a soft peony blush in the moonlight.

When she took his hands, the music began. They danced across the grass, under the willows, slowly at first. The girl was graceful, light in his arms.

Then with each measure the tempo grew faster. The girl's hair swirled out behind her, around them as they turned. She laughed with delight. She smelled like peonies.

A bit breathless, she said, "You dance well."

"With you anyone could dance well," he replied, surprised at his own boldness.

The music slowed. The girl held herself at arm's length as if to look better at him. "I could stay here always . . . if you know the magic and say it."

Again the tempo picked up; again he whirled with the girl in his arms.

"Magic?" Will tried to slow their dance. For a moment he and the girl stood in one spot marking time. He had to look at her. "Of course! I'll say it. Tell me what to say!" Will insisted.

"If you say it," the girl repeated, "I can stay here. If not, I'll change. In each form I take, I can remain here . . . *if* you know the magic and say it."

If he knew the magic. Of course he would say it. He would do anything to keep her here. She spoke as if he should know it.

"Please." Will rushed to speak while the music drove them ever faster across the grass. "If you can't tell me the magic I must know to keep you here, can you take me with you?"

Sadly she shook her head, then buried it in his shoulder. "Say the magic and I can stay," she whispered. Desperately, Will held the girl close to him.

Faster, faster went the music, until they whirled in a silver light.

Then,

Gone.

Girl and light and music were gone. Will lost his balance, fell on the grass. Into his arms leaped a kitten, black with willow-green eyes. It purred affectionately. Will stroked it.

"You'll go away too because I don't know the magic?" he murmured.

There they sat in the silver night. The kitten's purring seemed to last only a moment before it too was gone.

In its place a young hawk sat on Will's wrist, its talons holding more gently than Will ever thought they could. Abruptly it flew straight up, high in the moonlight, then back down, again landing so gently that Will felt only a small scratch, a few drops of blood on his hand.

Will was sad, sad to know that the hawk with its willow-green eyes would, like the others, leave him alone beside the stream. "If I knew the magic," he whispered to it, stroking its head with one finger. The bird blinked and was gone.

"How could the spring night be so full of magic, and I so ignorant, so empty?"

When he turned, there on the grass lay the silver fish.

"At least," said Will, "I can put you back to swim again." But the fish was dead, and seeing it there in the moonlight Will at last knew what he must do.

After gathering dry wood, he used his willow wand for a spit. Will cleaned and broiled the silver fish until it was perfect. Alone, Will sat by the stream to eat. With each bite the magic in him grew stronger.

"I am ready," he said aloud to the spring moonlight.

Family Vacation

"*Oh, goody* goody gopherguts, vacation!" sang Belinda Plummet as she closed the car door behind her.

"Yeah, Pops! Where are we going?" asked Thomas Plummet, leaning forward over the front seat.

Father Plummet glanced with momentary disapproval at his son. "Your language!" he admonished. Then, beaming, Father Plummet opened out the map.

"It's north this year, my little chickadees. Here. I've drawn the route."

"Thank goodness it's not south," sighed Belinda. "I hated going to the Fargos' last summer. It was grossly primitive. Remember? Remember how they said they lived off the land?"

Mother Plummet nodded over her crocheting. "Indeed I do. Wild-mushroom spaghetti sauce one night and those bony fish they caught for two nights, and then leftovers. Ugh! And Father had taken such trouble to learn where they had rented."

"Yes," sighed Father Plummet. "We nearly had to cut that visit short, and after we had driven such a long way. It's good we stayed one more day, though." He chuckled. "They finally did go to the grocery store. Our farewell dinner was splendid."

"They only shopped because they thought we had gone," sniffed Mother Plummet.

"Now Mother, that was last year. We are heading north now. From the grocery clerk I found out that the Harrigans have rented on Cape Cod. We'll drop in on them first."

"Goodie!" sang Belinda.

"From there we'll look up the . . ."

"Can't we go see Mr. Capet?" interrupted Thomas. "He's a swell cook and he has a sailboat."

"I'd love to, Thomas. I finally came right out and asked him about his summer plans. He was, well, he wouldn't tell, and he even resisted giving us the keys to his cabin. I'd say he is out for this year."

"It wouldn't do, anyway, if he's not there to cook," added Mother.

Then, in general happy agreement, the Plummets drove off into the summer morning. They had a most successful, most restful two weeks. As was their habit, they dropped in for a day or two or for three or four with every neighbor or acquaintance they had been able to find vacationing up north that summer.

The Plummets' skill in ferreting out the most closely guarded vacation secrets was legendary in their little town. For years it had been their custom to vacation in this manner, which often, however, required long, dull drives home. Then, after a simple request made by Mother Plummet one summer evening, the quality of their vacations improved and the Plummets introduced delightful strangers into their lives. "Dear," Mother

Plummet had said that summer evening, "dear. I'm tired." She put down the crocheting she always did in the car and whenever there were dishes to be washed. "I really do not want to shop for food when we arrive home. Nor do I want to cook dinner. Here we are, tired and hungry, driving through all of northern New Jersey, and at nearly every house we pass, someone is cooking a perfectly lovely dinner on an outdoor grill. All these barbecues smell so good. Can't we eat?"

Thomas sniffed the air loudly. "Can't we, Pops?"

"Oh, could we just stop and join someone?" sighed Belinda, beginning to comb her hair.

"No sooner said than done!" said Father Plummet. With that, he drove the car into the driveway of the next family they saw cooking outside.

"Hello! Hello! Bet you thought we'd be late!" cried Father Plummet, leaping from the car and bounding across the grass with vigor. You'd never have imagined that he had just driven two hundred miles that day. Joyfully he hugged the startled man and woman who stood at the picnic table.

"Dear, dear, oh how are you, dear?" smiled Mother Plummet. After kissing the air beside their hosts' bewildered heads, she sank into a lawn chair and began to crochet and chat while everyone waited on her.

"How's your summer been? Ours was great! You look terrific! Gosh, I'm thirsty!" shouted Thomas, helping himself to a soft drink.

"Me too," giggled Belinda. "See, I got my braces off!"

During dinner their hosts held at least one whispered

conversation in which words like "who," "where," and "mistake," occurred. After dinner the Plummets graciously helped clear the table before thanking their hosts profusely and driving the rest of the way home.

"They were nice," said Belinda. "Let's visit them again."

"We'll see dear," promised Father Plummet.

Those barbecue visits were wonderful. Afterward, refreshed and rested from their vacation, the Plummets arrived home. When the Plummets were particularly travel-worn, they even showered and changed their clothes before their astonished hosts had served them dinner and seen them depart.

This year, however, the Plummets have not been on vacation. Since May they have been kept at home by an uninterrupted succession of unexpected guests.

Father Plummet is gray and worn. But today at last he believes he has discovered the source of these surprise visitors. He found a printed flyer in the pocket of a pair of jeans he was folding for one of the guests. Father Plummet read the flyer even though it had been through both washer and dryer. Oh, how it hurt Father Plummet to spend all that money on electricity to dry those clothes. He was, however, forced by circumstances to do it. Today it rained, a hard, driving rain, and without dry clothes the guests would never have left.

Carefully Father Plummet unfolded the flyer. It was faded, but legible. *It invited all who had ever been visited by the Plummets to drop in on them for an indefinite stay.* The flyer gave clear and accurate directions to their little home, and it boasted that someone had copied down the license number of the Plummets' car one summer evening during a delicious barbecue dinner.

Tonight in bed, for the first time in weeks, Father Plummet smiles.

"I think, dear Mother," he says, "that it is time to sell our charming little house and move to the Southwest. The climate there is fine, and people barbecue all year round."

The Last Word

The car approached. Lola recognized the type, a car full of boys, out driving through the city, looking for excitement, for girls, for life. Anything would do; taunting an old lady would do.

There. The car slowed to a crawl. One boy grinned out at her, others were behind him, intent, listening. "Where are you going, ugly old woman?" he shouted.

"To marry your father, so that at last you will have a mother who is human!" Lola shot back.

The boys suddenly realized who she was. Pounding one another in glee, they drove away.

By morning Lola's latest retort would be known all over the city. She was always quoted with obvious delight in every café, as the coffee essence was poured into sticky glasses. Her barbed responses were whispered in the churches, while the vultures circled slowly around the bell towers. Everyone on the broad, treeless *avenidas* knew of Lola's tongue. Lola, whose word was always best, always last.

Lola had not always been so talented, so respected for her wit. As a child she had silently admired the quick ones, those who were clever with words. If Lola thought of the good retort, it was hours, days, weeks later, too late.

But Lola found she possessed an incredible memory. She remembered the quick responses, the clever ones made by others, and Lola worked hard at repartee. Slowly, almost imperceptibly, she discovered what to say. Sometimes she simply remembered and replied appropriately; sometimes she was brilliantly original. At first she formed those pithy responses only in her mind, but then Lola found her tongue.

Once she did, the results surprised and pleased her. At first within the city, and then throughout the country, she was known, respected, then feared. In a country where gossip and repartee were as necessary to life as food and drink, Lola had the last word.

That last word was not always cruel, or even unkind. She devastated those who attacked her, or any defenseless person within her hearing. Often, especially as age mellowed her, she was generous with a skilled turn of phrase that saved an awkward situation. One thing was certain: she did always have the last word, even if it was merely good-bye.

While she was still young and graceful, her grandmother, who had come down to the city from the high mountains many years before, tried to warn her of the dangers inherent for a girl with a mind too quick to find fault and a tongue too quick to expose it. Grandmother was, after all, old-fashioned, and she hoped Lola would curb her wit and tongue, and marry.

"Lola, you frighten the young men, and you *are* too

choosy. Remember, if you go through the forest looking for a stick that is not crooked, and throw away each one as you find it, you will reach the end of the forest empty-handed."

"Ah, Grandmother. The forest is far away," shrugged Lola. Her response may have been careless and not particularly witty, but it was the last word on the subject, for her grandmother died soon afterward and Lola never did marry.

Lola lived on and on and on, her reputation like that of a gunslinger. People came to challenge her. Lola always won.

One such opponent, one Lola scarcely noticed at the time, stood, quaking with fury after their exchange. His lips flecked with foam, he shouted a curse at Lola. "You will not die so long as you have the last word!"

"Amen," laughed Lola. Her large eyes, which were very beautiful, glittered. She was still young. What had she to fear? But that was years ago, long years before Lola knew the true meaning of the curse. Today Lola stood on the corner under that gray sky that never rained, leaning on her cane, waiting. If a bus or *colectivo* taxi came past, she would take it. She had money today. But if none came she could simply open the door of the first car that stopped for the traffic light and ask to be driven home. It was, after all, not far out of anyone's way, and it was known that Lola made such requests.

Everyone in the city knew of Lola, but by now everyone Lola had known was dead. She had been retired from her teaching at the university since before anyone now alive in the city was born. That thought came to her rather too often these past days. Lola was doing something she did not like to do. She was increasingly feeling sorry for herself.

No cars came. Lola stumped another long block. She sighed. She was alone. No great-grandchildren would mourn her. No one would light candles or pray for her. Ah yes, she could pay to have a mass or two said for her soul. But what matter if she could not die.

At home, Lola put down her string bag. Why on earth had she bought that fruit? Food no longer interested her. Days ago she had made up her mind. It had only been a question of how.

Slowly Lola moved the furniture out of the one room she now occupied in the moldy dark house. Out, out into the corridor went the books, all of them. Out went the heavy, dark wardrobe, the table, the chairs, everything but her bed. It took most of the night. No matter. She rarely slept. Lola swept the room clean, made up the bed.

"Now it looks like a nun's cell. It is a fit room for dying." Lola had made up her mind, but dying was not so easy. Her first idea had been to go out into the city on her daily business and, when she was addressed, simply not to answer. If she did not speak she could not have the last word. There would be a certain drama in dying out in the world. The idea had appealed to her for about a day. But then dying was not easy. Three things stopped her.

The Last Word

There were the polite people. They greeted her, "Good morning, Señora Lola."

Lola, courteous, automatically replied in kind. Hah! Even "good morning" could be a curse.

Then there were the idiots. If someone says something incorrect or just plain silly, how can a decent, intelligent person not speak to correct it? That was a problem for Lola.

Then, finally, there was dignity. If she did curb her tongue and deny herself the last word, could an old lady fall dead on the street with her skirts flying above her ankles, and perhaps saliva drooling from cracked lips? It would never do.

Lola finally decided that she would have to die alone in her room. She had decided. She had prepared the room. Now Lola lay down to wait.

Lola knew she might have to wait a long time. Had she not had the last word just a few hours ago on the street? She had.

Lola practiced, in her mind, not answering. She practiced dying. Lola lay and waited, with a little fear growing in her heart. No one would come. She would lie there, alive, forever, because no one would come to say the last word.

Just when she was certain that she had failed, there was a knock on the door.

At first Lola did not answer. She lay there thinking that surely the person would come in, speak, and Lola could remain silent, and die.

Bah! The knocking ceased. Lola grew more afraid.

Ah, the person will leave. I will not die. Attempting to sound weak, and still to be heard through the thick door, Lola croaked, "Enter." No one answered. The door remained shut.

Ah. I must leave the door open. Lola got out of bed and opened the door. No one was there. She returned to bed.

Bang!

Never before had a breeze blown that door shut. Lola got up again, propped the door open with a large dictionary, and returned to bed to wait.

Much later a young girl appeared at the door. Lola tried to look sick. She must have succeeded, for the girl's face went very white. "Señora Lola!" It was the girl from the fruit stand where Lola bought fruit every day. Of course, that girl would notice; she was kind. How good of her to come. The girl touched Lola's hand. Lola smiled.

"Shall I call a doctor?"

Lola blinked.

"Oh. I'll call a doctor. . . ."

Poor child; she was upset. Lola wanted to reassure her, tried to look encouraging. The girl took Lola's cold, dry little hands into her own warm ones. "Yes . . . ," the girl whispered, "and a priest."

Lola smiled. Finally things were going in the correct manner. Twice she had not answered. Lola was sure she felt death coming for her. The girl ran away. Lola smiled. Now. Surely now she could die. She had not spoken.

The Last Word

Some time later, Lola awoke with a start. Was nothing ever to end? She must have dozed off, for this most assuredly was not death. The room was full of people, including a doctor who held her wrist, the girl from the fruit stand, others, and a young priest with the most vacuous face Lola had ever seen. Where on earth had they found him? He wasn't from this parish. And what was he saying? Not simple prayers for the dying as he should, but making a speech, the kind of platitudes heard at the funerals of strangers. Where were the priests from this parish? Where?

Lola bit her tongue. I must not speak. The phrase repeated itself inside her head.

Someone, perhaps angel, perhaps devil, who appears to be a fool has been sent to tempt me. But I'll not give in, not this time.

"It must be a stroke." Everyone in the room was watching her, whispering back and forth. "See. She cannot reply, but oh, what she would tell that foolish priest prattling on over her! Look how her eyes flash."

Lola closed her eyes, shut out the voices, concentrated on the bells that had begun to ring the Angelus throughout the city. When all the other bells had finished, one lingered on.

"Ahhhhhh," sighed the people in the room. "Listen. It is Lola."

Gentle hands made the sign of the cross on her. Lola smiled. The test must be over. She had not spoken. They had named a bell for her. I must not speak.

Lola held her breath for that last Amen.

AFTERWORD

From a Storyteller

Yesterday my daughter mentioned an article she had read in the newspaper. "A little boy discovered a python in the toilet," she told me. "Really?" I asked. "What city was this in? What newspaper?" "I don't remember exactly," she said, "but it really happened." Can you imagine what Judith Gorog could do with an item like that? I'll bet she could fashion a tale to remember, and include it in a book just like this one.

In fact, if you look through this book a second time, you'll find the author used various sources from her own experiences to create these bizarre but believably realistic stories. At least three of them have their roots in story-swapping sessions around campfires in the Adirondack mountains. You've probably already guessed that "Dr. Egger's Favorite Dog," "Hookman" and "No Swimming in Dark Pond" might have been shared in the night with just the light of a fire casting eerie shadows on the faces of the listeners. For others, like "Flawless Beauty" and "How I Kill My Step-mothers," the author undoubtedly relied on her reading (both as a child and as an adult) of traditional fairy tales. Yet another genre she may have read is reflected in "Nemesis," "Tim the Alien" and "The Notebook." These stories can be categorized as fantasy or its cousin, science fiction.

Professional folklorists might find yet another tale-type in this collection, what we call the Urban Tale. This is a story that sounds like the folktales of old, but with a city or suburban setting. It is the kind of story my daughter related to me. These tales are usually frag-mented, and mostly plot—"A python in the toilet!"—with little characterization or setting. An author such as Judith Gorog takes an incident (true or maybe not-so-true) and imagines what went before, and what might have happened after, the "shocking moment." "Mr. Randolph" and "Family Vacation" are fine examples of this type of story.

However, while the forms of stories in a Judith Gorog book might be familiar, the tales themselves often take an unexpected turn. For instance, in "How I Kill My Stepmothers" it is the stepchild rather than the step-mother who is really wicked. The unexpected is Judith Gorog's trademark. That is what makes these tales chill-ing. There is nothing quite so spine-tingly and thrilling as a scary story.

So, if you are interested in sharing these stories with your friends, why not try telling them? You'll have to do a little preparation if you want to sound convincing. Simply read the story of your choice through two or three times, imagining the action taking place as pic-tures in your mind. Next, begin to tell the story to your-self until you're confident that you can make it sound as natural and as current as telling someone about what you did last weekend. Then practice on someone at home, your mom or even your dog. When you feel you're ready for the big debut, dim the lights (or turn them off) and share a scary story with your friends.

Dr. Caroline Bauer